I0699132

JOURNAL *of the* WESTBRAE LITERARY GROUP

Issue 2, Winter 2025

Berkeley, Calif.
2024

ISBN 979-8-9917199-3-3
Published by Westbrae Literary Group
Berkeley, California

EDITOR

Jon-David Hague, Founding Editor

JOURNAL OF THE WESTBRAE LITERARY GROUP

Published semi-regularly by Westbrae Literary Group, promoting authors who bring fresh, raw voices to the forefront of American literature. We are dedicated to publishing work that challenges the traditional canon, offering a platform to writers with unique and authentic perspectives.

SUBMISSIONS

Westbrae Literary Group accepts rolling submissions year-round. We welcome work in the following categories: **Essays, Poetry, Art, Short Stories, Excerpts from Prose in Progress and Forthcoming**

Please submit manuscripts via email to submissions@westbraeliterarygroup.com. Include a brief cover letter and biography with your submission.

CONTACT INFORMATION
Westbrae Literary Group
info@westbraeliterarygroup.com
westbraeliterarygroup.com

CONTENTS

CONTRIBUTORS

Dustin Anderson is a passionate storyteller and dedicated father of five—two sons and three daughters. He and his wife live in Bloomington, Indiana, where they raise their kids; the town where Dustin too was raised.

David Dephy is an American award-winning poet, novelist, essayist, multi-media artist, with a Master of Fine Arts degree evaluated by the Globe Language USA. The founder of Poetry Orchestra and American Poetry Intersection. Poet-in-Residence for Brownstone Poets 2024-2025. His poem, "A Sense of Purpose," is being sent to the Moon by The Lunar Codex, NASA, and Brick Street Poetry in 2024. He is named as "A Literature Luminary" by Bowery Poetry and "Stellar Poet" by Voices of Poetry. He was exiled from his native country of Georgia in 2017 and was granted political asylum in the USA. His family, beloved wife and 9-year-old son joined him in the U.S. after 7 years of exile in 2023. He lives and works in New York City.

Josh Greenbaum has been writing poetry and assorted prose-like stuff for decades, specializing largely in unpublished works. When not braving the streets of Berkeley on his bike, he can be found hiking, breathing fresh air, and cooking. He writes at the Left Margin Lit writers' workshop, where he is currently working on his first unpublished novel, an excerpt from which will be published in the next JWLG.

Michael Ryle was born in Atlanta and grew up in the South. After a stint in the US Army in Germany, he graduated from the University of Tennessee with a degree in English, intending to teach, but unexpected opportunities led him to pursue a career in music, playing jazz with such artists as Jim Hall and Jerry Coker and classical with Rudolf Nureyev, Joshua Bell and Yo-Yo Ma. He worked as a software engineer in Connecticut for a number of years and then moved to Cape Cod where he put together a patchwork of jobs in business management, music performance, and composing and arranging in order to focus on writing. His short stories have appeared in Brilliant Corners and The Cape Cod Literary Journal. Since experimenting with verse a little over year ago, he has changed to writing poetry exclusively.

Mandy Tripp is a San Francisco-based artist specializing in geometric pen and ink illustrations for over a decade. A self-taught creator, Mandy began her artistic journey in 2012, initially drawing mandalas as a form of personal therapy, despite having little prior experience with art. Since then, she has dedicated herself to refining her craft, drawing inspiration from her surroundings and the work of fellow artists.

Nichole Turnbloom is a poet, yoga therapist, amateur potter and workshop facilitator. She currently works for a nonprofit where she provides individual and small groups sessions to those affected by trauma and violence. She has an MFA in poetry and has been published in Acumen 108 and other online venues.

EDITOR'S NOTE

A serendipitous thread woven through this second issue of *JWLG* is the resonance of the ancient Greek poet Sappho. Two poets, submitting independently, have been inspired by her verses. Their works echo her themes and enter a dialogue with her—bridging millennia to explore love, identity, and the short moments of beauty that define our lives. I've included the Greek text of Sappho and the fragments alongside translations, one of which is mine.

David Dephy's poems bring a strong sense of place, of moment, that hit at the connection of time and memory, in lines that weave streams of consciousness.

This issue also features contributions that delve into contemporary explorations of self and society. From a short story that captures the intersection of the extraordinary and the mundane to artwork that seems to breathe through the pages, each piece is a world unto itself, yet part of a larger conversation. The excerpt from *Coyote and Crow Save the World* offers a tantalizing glimpse into a universe where myth and reality collide.

Thank you for being a part of this journey.

Jon-David Hague
Berkeley, Calif. January 2025

POETRY

Sappho Poem 1
Hymn to Aphrodite[1]

trans. Jon-David Hague

Flower-crowned deathless Aphrodite,
Zeus's child, weaver of deceits, I pray:
don't crush my heart with pain, my queen.

But come here now like you've done before
when you heard me and left your father's
golden halls and came

riding in your sparrow-drawn chariot,
their wings thick over the dark earth
from heaven down to me

in an instant they came and you,
happy, smiled your god smile and asked
why I was suffering again and why was I
calling you again

and what was it my wild heart wanted:
"Who do I again convince to return to your arms?
Who's done you wrong,
Sappho?

---

[1] This is a complete poem of Sappho (Greek from Lesbos, born 610 BCE, died 570 BCE). Dionysius of Halicarnassus quotes the poem. We also have bits of it on a worn, worm-eaten papyrus from the 100s CE. Hear the poem in ancient Greek on Spotify at *Poetae Graeci et Latini* (recited not sung to music). Line 19 in the Greek (see below) has crosses (cruces) because scholars think Dionysius's text there is wrong. My rendering of the Greek at 19 is my own.

If she's shunning you, soon she won't.
If she's not taking your gifts, she'll give them.
If she doesn't love you, soon she will,
whether she wants to or not."

Just come here now. Get rid of this pain.
Everything my heart wants, give me.
Be my ally in love.

Sappho's Greek, Poem 1

ποικιλόθρον’ ἀθανάτ’ Ἀφρόδιτα,
παῖ Δίος δολόπλοκε, λίσσομαί σε,
μή μ’ ἄσαισι μηδ’ ὀνίαισι δάμνα,
πότνια, θῦμον·

ἀλλὰ τυίδ’ ἔλθ’, αἴ ποτα κἀτέρωτα
τὰς ἔμας αὔδας ἀίοισα πήλοι
ἔκλυες, πάτρος δὲ δόμον λίποισα
χρύσιον ἦλθες

ἄρμ’ ὑπασδεύξαισα· κάλοι δέ σ’ ἆγον
ὤκεες στροῦθοι περὶ γᾶς μελαίνας
πύκνα δίννεντες πτέρ’ ἀπ’ ὠράνωἴθε-
ρος διὰ μέσσω·

αἶψα δ’ ἐξίκοντο· σὺ δ’, ὦ μάκαιρα,
μειδιαίσαισ’ ἀθανάτῳ προσώπῳ
ἤρε’ ὄττι δηῦτε πέπονθα κὤττι
δηῦτε κάλημμι

κὤττι μοι μάλιστα θέλω γένεσθαι
μαινόλᾳ θύμῳ· τίνα δηῦτε πείθω
†ἄψ ἄγην ἐς σὰν† φιλότατα; τίς σ’, ὦ
Ψάπφ’, ἀδικήει;

καὶ γὰρ αἰ φεύγει, ταχέως διώξει,
αἰ δὲ δῶρα μὴ δέκετ’, ἀλλὰ δώσει,
αἰ δὲ μὴ φίλει, ταχέως φιλήσει
κωὐκ ἐθέλοισα."

ἔλθε μοι καὶ νῦν, χαλέπαν δὲ λῦσον
ἐκ μερίμναν, ὄσσα δέ μοι τέλεσσαι
θῦμος ἰμέρρει, τέλεσον, σὺ δ’ αὔτα
σύμμαχος ἔσσο.

Michael Ryle

from *The Braeland Poems: Soliloquies*

(forthcoming from Westbrae Literary Group)

iv. (after Sappho, Poem 1)

She's been to the finest spas, around the world —
Dubai, for the placenta facials,
Hong Kong, for ultrasonic collagen,
hammams and Vichy showers in Marrakech,
Himalayan abhyanga oil massage,
microneedle wands of foreskin stem cells,
blood platelets, bee venom, goldleaf—

Yet, in a pinch, I'm the one she calls.

"Come to me, Vaness, her message reads,
or else you'll crush my spirit like a petal.
If ever I could count on you before,
I need you now. I'm in an awful place—
my cave drips with pain."

         That's my Dora,
drama queen, without a doubt, but still
my best client. She's been with me forever.
Mother, sister, best friend, I'm a little
of all three to her.

                "The tour from Hell
ends tonight in Milan," she writes,
"and after that I never want to sing
a note or finger a guitar again.
Even now, as I tap these words,
my chariot with flocks of sparrows painted
on the wings jets the ocean toward
the Evening Star on its way to you.
Your private cabin's filled with fresh-cut flowers,
silken pillows, finest linens, stars
stippled on the ceiling. My limousine
will be waiting for you at the airport.
We'll go shopping at La Galleria,
run like children through the Liberty Fountain,
go to Brera, snicker at *Il Bacio*,
sprawl out on the terrace while the brook
whispers gossip through the apple blossoms.
I know I ask a lot, for you to drop
what you're doing now and come to me,
you possessing everything and knowing
everything, but if you're here with me
I know I cannot fail."

                Oh, my goodness,
dearest Dora, what's the matter now?
What absconded lover must I restore
to your arms, *this* time? What goes on
in that crazy, crazy heart of yours?
She falls, and every time she's off and
running like a filly in a springtime meadow.
A lovely face, a coy look withdrawn,
her joints melt, her heart palpitates,

her eyes shellac, her ears jangle, the sweat
pours, she's wet as the morning dew.

She loves as if love's the only thing
on earth, the careless ones who treat her worst
and leave her grasping after with her spirit
like an oak tree hammered by the wind,
a monster with a hundred waving arms.

Whoever's wronged her now, I suspect
it's someone younger. Dora's not so old
herself, but she feels it, and she thinks
that I have swindles up my sleeve to make
the girl relent, that I can soften her
like the callus on a foot, and if
she's not in love, she will be when I'm done.

Well, skin I know, and hair and nails, and scrubs,
massage, meditation, mindfulness,
nutrition, circulation, general wellness,
all the paths to the happy hormones.
If it buys her a night of feeling
loved, the money is well-spent, I think.

Yet the truth is, all you have to do
is bind her balayage in a purple
headband, sit her down with her guitar
and listen to her sing her songs, and you
will think, here's someone who's found a purl
in time, who'll never grow a moment older.

Dora, dearest love, of course I'll come.

Nichole Turnbloom

Watching my Two Daughters at the Same Event, Ten Years Apart

I used to weave crowns
with delicate white daisies
while sitting on a knoll through
the long days of summer

and later with seed beads
through fishing line as gifts for friends

and later still with raffia braided
I wove delicate baby breath, with blush rose
Spanish lavender with young branches of rosemary into
crowns that bloomed with soft petals scented
to watch as my daughters danced and weaved
with ribbon, over and under, around one another
as they wove bold lines of
blue, purple, red and yellow
into patterns around the Maypole.

I have darned holes
stitched alibis with fingers crosses
interlaced stories with movement,
spun webs into castles

sometimes out of nothing--
with nothing but silence,

and now I am like Penelope
unweaving by the moonlight
under and over, searching for
the lost thread to pull myself through.

*Italic line is Sappho fragment 125 (following Anne Carson, *If Not, Winter* who follows Eva-Maria Voigt's Greek text):

†αυταόρα† ἐστεφαναπλόκην

Editor's note: we have this line of Greek because an ancient commentator on the play *Thesmophoriazusae* (Women at the Thesmophoria Festival) by Aristophanes (famed Greek comic playwright of the later 400s BCE) quotes it at line 400. †αυταόρα† is unattested elsewhere. It might be a combination of the words for "self" and "time when one is young". So, a possible translation could be "I used to weave crowns myself when I was young."

Jacqueline

You only appear *small*.
A lonely lighthouse illuminating
rocky contours, and *many*
heed your warning: change

course, *many*
more like dropped stitches *their*
lives swallowed whole
by the sea. And all you taste
is saline. All you feel
is the wind of *Gorgo*
stinging eyes. And all
I see is light.

*Italics are Sappho fragment 103Aa (Carson and Voigt see above)

σμικρ[
τὰν σφ[
πολλα[
   πρὶγ γα[

πόλλαισ[
τῶν σφω[ν
ὠδαμελ[
   χει[

Γοργ[

Mythweaver

"We have lived our death a thousand times"
— Robert Bly

And the children wait unmanifested

on the horizon of Gaia's inner eye,

the waterline thick with kohl

eyes unblinking

black as the mouth of color before it speaks.

Sleep as once upon a time, sleep as millions

of years of evolution in an hour.

Night only pretends to close its eyes, waits for dawn.

*Title of poem is Sappho Fragment 188 (just one word):
μυθόπλοκος

This poem is a reverse golden shovel (a golden shovel ends lines)
with Sappho fragment 151 (just five words): ὀφθάλμοις δὲ μέλαις
νύκτος ἄωρος (*lit.* and on black eyes night's sleep)

David Dephy

from *Rays Never Were So Near as Now* (forthcoming)

Time Is Up

Night tells us who's most precious,
most close—
which reflection most resembles our hearts.

Night has a heart of a prophet.

When we were young and went to that garden,
we saw the silkworm, but time is up,
it is a butterfly now.

Forest

Sick of the illusions raised by the killers,
became teachers.

Sick of the dust raised by those teachers,
became fools.

On the edge of the past, the fears are rolling over.
We are still running all around each other

in forest and its dark stillness. A stillness never
tells
the truth. Forest is only a body of leaf's soul.

We still believe the war is over now, but do not
recall
who won it. Kind people, no doubt, for only they

would leave so many dead. Their last breath
keeps us turning back to something forgotten,

to something misplaced, keeps us turning
back toward their dreams, which are blameless.

A Bird Above New York City

The sky is getting closer with every breath.
I found everything when I found myself.
I am enough to the world.

The winds are running air, reside earth,
each in its own way, they are beauty of the world,
they are enough as they are.

I flew away from the nest directly to your heart,
air,
you are enough — my mother sky, and I am
getting
closer to you and closer,

into your arms I feel myself naked and free.
I feel strange when I look up to the sky.
Above me is a golden silence of my own
expectations.

Maybe this man thinks he also can fly, maybe that
one
tree knows the truth about all the locations of the
oldest
treasures buried deep in the ground, and I am still
looking

up to the sky where the seagull is chasing the
breeze and
laughingly cries, when the morning relieves,
silently reveals all the mysteries of the night
when constellations were high.

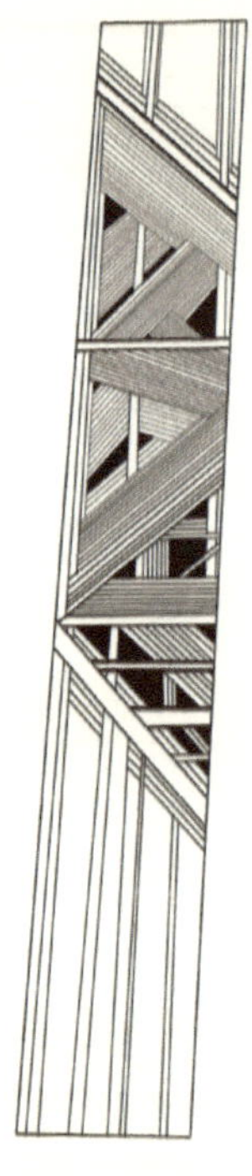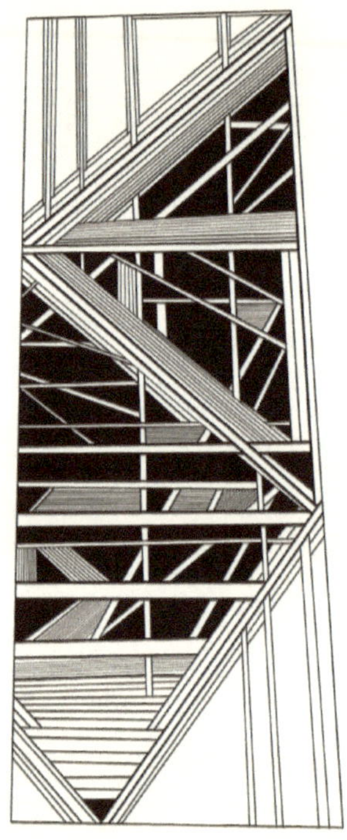

Prose
Short Stories

Dustin Anderson

The Unified Theory

Chapters 1 to 5

Chapter 1: The Quiet Mechanic

Mark Henderson wiped the grease from his hands, staring out of the garage window as the last hint of daylight faded behind the rooftops of his small Ohio neighborhood. It had been a long day—a series of tune-ups and oil changes, the occasional brake repair. The kind of monotonous work that paid the bills but left his mind restless. He locked the shop doors and sighed, the familiar ache in his back from bending over engines all day now an ever-present companion.

Home was just a short drive away, but the weight of fatherhood, responsibility, and endless chores made each step toward his car feel like a hike up a mountain. Five kids awaited him. Five sets of homework, dinner preparations, bedtimes. The house would be alive with noise and chaos— spilled milk, raised voices, and the background hum of the TV competing with children asking questions about math problems and spelling tests.

And yet, despite the exhaustion, Mark felt a small flicker of excitement deep inside him. Later, after the children were in bed, when the house was finally quiet, he would have his time. Time to escape into numbers, to puzzle through equations that held the key to mysteries far beyond his daily grind.

It had always been like this for him. Mathematics had been his private sanctuary since he was young—a secret language that whispered promises of understanding the universe's greatest questions. He had been good at it, too. So good, in fact, that his professors in college had encouraged him to pursue a career in theoretical physics. But that had been years ago, before Sarah, before the kids, before life.

Mark had dropped out of college when Sarah got pregnant with their first child. The decision had been easy at the time—his family needed him, and theoretical physics didn't exactly offer a reliable paycheck. He had promised himself that he'd return to it one day, when things were more stable. But with each passing year, that promise felt more and more distant, the dream slowly fading into the background.

Now, though, it was different. Something had reignited his passion for the subject. Over the past few months, Mark had found himself diving deeper into astrophysics, specifically into the study of black holes. He had been reading about them for years, fascinated by their ability to bend spacetime, their event horizons beyond which nothing—not even light—could escape. But recently, he had started to see connections he hadn't seen before, mathematical patterns that hinted at something more profound.

He had been scribbling equations in an old notebook after the kids went to bed, slowly piecing together a theory. It was still rough, incomplete, but it felt significant. He wasn't just studying black holes anymore; he was starting to believe that black holes weren't just destructive forces—they were central to the very fabric of the universe.

Mark had come to a startling realization: what if everything, all matter and energy, was fundamentally made up of black holes? What if black holes, in different dimensions and at different scales, were the building blocks of existence itself? Stars, planets, atoms, even life— all connected by the same universal principle of collapse and expansion. Everything could be in a constant state of flux, like a cosmic heartbeat—a cycle of collapse into singularities, followed by expansion into new forms.

This idea had consumed Mark for weeks now, haunting his thoughts even as he went through the motions of his daily life. It wasn't just idle speculation; the math supported it, or at least he thought it did. The equations weren't complete, but every time he worked on them, they seemed to converge toward something bigger—something more profound than any single theory in modern physics. He called it the "Unified Theory of Infinite Dimensionality and Collapse-Expansion Dynamics."

It was a mouthful, and Mark knew that if he ever shared it with anyone, he'd have to come up with a simpler name. But for now, it was his secret, something he wasn't quite ready to share with the world. Part of him wasn't even sure if it was real. How could someone like him—a mechanic with no formal degree, no connections in academia—stumble upon the key to understanding the universe?

He pulled into the driveway of his modest home, the noise from inside already spilling out into the street. The front door opened before he even reached it, and his youngest daughter,

Penny, came bounding out, her face lit with excitement.

"Daddy!" she yelled, throwing her arms around his waist. "Guess what? I got a star on my spelling test!"

Mark scooped her up into his arms, kissing her on the forehead. "A star? That's amazing, Penny! You're getting smarter every day."

Penny beamed, and for a moment, Mark allowed himself to be fully present, to forget about black holes and equations, and just enjoy the simple joy of being a father.

Inside, Sarah was wrangling their other four children, trying to get dinner on the table amidst the chaos. Mark kissed her cheek as he passed by, giving her a tired smile.

"Long day?" she asked, her voice heavy with the kind of exhaustion only parents of young children know.

"You have no idea," Mark replied, grabbing a plate and helping himself to the spaghetti she had made. "But we got through it."

They ate together as a family, the conversation light and filled with the usual chatter about school and friends. But Mark's mind was only half in the room. The equations, the theory— they gnawed at the edges of his thoughts, pulling him away even as he tried to stay grounded in the moment.

Later that night, after the kids were asleep and the house was finally quiet, Mark retreated to his small office in the basement. It wasn't much— just a desk, an old lamp, and a few shelves filled with books on mathematics and physics. His notebook lay open on the desk, the pages filled with scribbled equations and diagrams.

He sat down and stared at the numbers, feeling that familiar rush of excitement. He was close, so close to something big. He could feel it in his bones. But there was still a gap in the equations, something missing that he couldn't quite pin down.

For hours, he worked in silence, pencil scratching against paper as he tried to make sense of the patterns. His eyes burned from the strain, but he didn't stop. Time blurred. Midnight came and went. The only sounds in the room were the steady ticking of the clock and the hum of the furnace.

And then, sometime in the early hours of the morning, it happened. Mark's hand froze in midair as a realization hit him with the force of a freight train.

He had been thinking about black holes in the wrong way. They weren't just singularities—isolated points of collapse. They were part of a larger structure, a network that spanned dimensions. In fact, the entire universe might be made up of interconnected black holes, each one collapsing and expanding in different ways across different dimensions.

His theory wasn't just about black holes—it was about the very nature of reality. The universe wasn't static; it was a living, breathing thing, constantly folding in on itself and expanding out again in a dance of infinite dimensionality. And at the heart of that dance were black holes, shaping and reshaping the cosmos in ways that defied conventional understanding.

Mark's heart raced as he scribbled down the final equation, the one that tied it all together. It was beautiful. Elegant. And, as far as he could tell, correct.

He sat back in his chair, staring at the equation in awe. This was it. The Unified Theory of Infinite Dimensionality and Collapse-Expansion Dynamics. It explained everything: the structure of the universe, the relationship between quantum mechanics and general relativity, the very nature of existence.

But as the initial rush of excitement faded, a new feeling crept in—fear. What if no one believed him? What if his theory was dismissed as the ramblings of an amateur with no formal training? He could barely afford the time he spent on this work as it was. If he shared it with the world, he would be opening himself up to ridicule, to rejection.

Still, Mark couldn't ignore the truth of what he had discovered. He knew, deep down, that this theory was important. It could change the way humanity understood the universe. He just had to find a way to share it with the right people.

Mark leaned back in his chair, rubbing his eyes. The fatigue was catching up with him now, but his mind was still buzzing with the implications of what he had just uncovered. He wasn't sure what to do next, but one thing was certain—his life was about to change forever.

<u>Chapter 2: An Unlikely Theorist</u>

In the days that followed, Mark couldn't shake the feeling that he had crossed a threshold, that he was standing on the edge of something monumental. He went to work, fixed cars, played with his kids, but his mind was constantly returning to the equations in his notebook. The theory was too big to keep to himself. He had to do something with it. But how?

He didn't know anyone in the academic world anymore. The professors he had studied under in college were long gone, and he had no connections in the field of theoretical physics. For all intents and purposes, Mark Henderson was a nobody—just a mechanic from Ohio with a wild idea about black holes and the structure of the universe.

But the more he thought about it, the more he realized that he couldn't let fear hold him back. He had to take a chance, to put his work out there and see if anyone would listen. After all, wasn't that what science was about—sharing ideas, challenging the status quo, pushing the boundaries of human understanding?

One evening, after the kids were in bed, Mark sat down at his computer and typed up a summary of his theory. He kept it simple, focusing on the key points—the idea that black holes were not just isolated singularities but the fundamental building blocks of the universe, the notion that collapse and expansion were part of a larger cosmic cycle, and the possibility that black holes operated across multiple dimensions.

When he was finished, he stared at the screen for a long time, his finger hovering over the "send" button. He had found the email addresses of a few professors at the local university's physics department, and he was about to send them his theory.

Would they even read it? Or would they dismiss it as the work of a crackpot? Mark wasn't sure, but he knew he had to try.

With a deep breath, he hit send.

And then he waited.

Days passed. Mark checked his email constantly, but there was no response. He tried to focus on his work, on his family, but the anxiety gnawed at him. What if he had made a mistake? What if his theory wasn't as solid as he thought?

And then, one evening, just as he was about to sit down to dinner, his phone buzzed. Mark glanced at the screen and saw an unfamiliar email address.

The subject line read: Re: Your Theory.

Mark's heart raced as he opened the email. It was short, just a few sentences, but the words sent a jolt of adrenaline through his body.

"Dear Mr. Henderson,

We have reviewed the summary of your theory. We would like to invite you to present it to our faculty. Please let us know if you are available to meet.

Best regards,

Dr. Jameson

Department of Physics, Ohio University."

Mark stared at the email, his hands trembling. They wanted to meet with him. They were taking him seriously.

He had done it. He had cracked open the door to a world he thought was closed to him forever. Now all he had to do was step through it.

Chapter 3: The Eureka Moment

Mark could hardly sleep that night. His mind was consumed with the thought of what lay ahead—his meeting with the physics faculty at Ohio University. He had re-read the email from Dr. Jameson a dozen times, each time feeling a surge of disbelief. They wanted to hear his theory. These were real physicists, experts in their field, and they were interested in what he had to say.

As the morning sun crept into the sky, Mark lay awake, staring at the ceiling. His excitement was shadowed by a deep sense of dread. What if they ripped his theory apart? What if, despite the math and the hours of late-night study, there was some fundamental flaw he had overlooked?

The morning passed in a blur of routine. He made breakfast for the kids, kissed Sarah goodbye, and set out for Ohio University. The drive there felt both too short and too long, his mind alternating between excitement and anxiety. By the time he pulled into the campus parking lot, his hands were clammy, and his heartbeat had quickened.

He had dressed in his best clothes—a suit jacket he hadn't worn since his cousin's wedding three years ago—and carried his well-worn notebook under one arm. The rest of the materials—printouts of his equations and diagrams—were stuffed into an old briefcase he had borrowed from his father.

Mark had visited the university only a few times before, mostly when his older kids had participated in science fairs, but today felt different. Today, he wasn't just an observer—he was presenting his work to people who had spent their entire lives in academia, people who had devoted themselves to the pursuit of knowledge. And here he was, a mechanic with no degree, about to explain the universe's mysteries.

The physics building loomed ahead of him, a sleek, modern structure with towering glass windows. Mark paused at the entrance, taking a deep breath before pushing the door open. Inside, students and faculty bustled through the hallways, their conversations filled with jargon he barely understood. Mark felt out of place, a visitor in a world that wasn't his.

"Mr. Henderson?"

Mark turned to see a tall man with graying hair and wire-rimmed glasses approaching him. His face was lined with age, but his eyes were sharp and focused.

"I'm Dr. Jameson," the man said, extending his hand. "Thank you for coming. We're very interested in what you've been working on."

Mark shook his hand, trying to hide the tremble in his fingers. "Thank you for inviting me. I— I didn't expect anyone to respond."

Dr. Jameson gave him a small, knowing smile. "We get a lot of wild theories from amateur scientists, but yours… well, there was something intriguing about it. Something we couldn't ignore."

Mark's heart raced as Dr. Jameson led him down a long hallway to a conference room where a group of professors waited. There were four of them in total, each representing a different area of expertise—cosmology, quantum mechanics, mathematical physics, and string theory. They greeted Mark politely, though their expressions were measured, clearly waiting to see what he had to offer.

The room was stark and professional. A projector hummed in the corner, and the walls were lined with bookshelves filled with volumes of academic texts. As Mark set up his notes, the professors watched him with quiet curiosity, their pens poised over their notebooks.

Dr. Jameson sat at the head of the table. "Whenever you're ready, Mr. Henderson." Mark took a deep breath and began.

He started slowly, outlining the basic principles of black holes—how they formed, their gravitational pull, the event horizon, and the singularity at their core. This was material the professors already knew, but Mark wanted to lay the foundation before diving into the more radical parts of his theory. He noticed a few nods of approval as he spoke, which gave him the confidence to continue.

Then, he moved on to the crux of his theory: the idea that black holes were not isolated anomalies in the universe, but fundamental building blocks that existed at every scale. He described how his equations pointed to the possibility that all matter and energy were governed by the same principles of collapse and expansion. Black holes, he argued, were central to this process—acting as nodes in an infinite web of dimensional interactions.

The room was silent as Mark spoke. He could see the professors exchanging glances, their faces gradually shifting from polite skepticism to genuine interest. Mark's voice grew stronger as he continued, explaining how black holes might exist not only in the large-scale structures of galaxies but also at the quantum level, influencing the behavior of particles and even the fabric of spacetime itself.

He showed them his equations—mathematical proofs that seemed to suggest that black holes could connect different dimensions, acting as portals or bridges between realities. It was bold, and Mark knew it. But the math was there, and the professors couldn't deny it.

As he reached the conclusion of his presentation, Mark felt a weight lift off his shoulders. He had laid everything out, held nothing back. Now it was up to them.

For a moment, the room was silent. Then Dr. Jameson leaned forward, his eyes fixed on Mark's notes.

"This is…astonishing," he said softly. "If your calculations hold up, this could be one of the most significant breakthroughs in our understanding of the universe."

Mark's breath caught in his throat. Was he hearing this right?

One of the other professors, Dr. Patel, nodded in agreement. "I have to admit, I was skeptical when I read your email. But the way you've tied black hole dynamics to both quantum mechanics and higher-dimensional theories… it's compelling. You've managed to bridge gaps that have baffled scientists for decades."

Mark could hardly believe it. They were taking him seriously.

"But," Dr. Patel continued, "this is still a preliminary framework. There's a lot more work to be done to refine the theory, to prove it conclusively."

Dr. Jameson nodded. "Agreed. Your equations are elegant, but we'll need to run them through peer review, to test them against current models. But I believe there's real potential here, Mr. Henderson. You've given us a lot to think about."

Mark felt lightheaded. He had hoped they might listen, that they wouldn't dismiss him outright. But this… this was more than he had ever imagined. They were talking about his theory as if it had real merit—as if it could change the field of physics.

Dr. Jameson leaned back in his chair, studying Mark for a moment. "Tell me, how did you come up with this?"

Mark hesitated, unsure of how to explain it. How could he tell them that his theory had come to him in the quiet hours after his kids were asleep, in the dim light of his basement office, where the hum of the furnace was his only company?

"I don't know," he finally said. "I just… I saw the connections. The equations, the patterns. It felt like they were leading me somewhere."

The professors exchanged glances again, this time with a hint of amusement.

"Sometimes," Dr. Patel said with a smile, "the most important discoveries come from places we least expect."

The meeting continued for another hour as the professors asked Mark questions, probing deeper into his theory. By the time it ended, Mark felt both exhilarated and exhausted. He had been able to answer most of their questions, though some required deeper thought, and he knew there were still gaps in his understanding. But they were treating him like an equal, like someone who belonged in the conversation.

As the meeting wound down, Dr. Jameson stood and extended his hand again. "Mr. Henderson, I think we're at the beginning of something significant here. We'll need to work closely to refine your theory, but I believe you've made a breakthrough. If you're open to it, we'd like to collaborate with you."

Mark stood there, stunned, as the professors around the room nodded in agreement. Collaborate? Him, the mechanic who studied late at night in his basement, was being asked to work alongside actual physicists? The surreal nature of the moment nearly overwhelmed him, but he managed to stammer out a response.

"I…I'd love to," Mark said, his voice unsteady. "Thank you. I can't believe this."

Dr. Jameson smiled. "Believe it. But be prepared—there's a lot of work ahead. We'll be in touch to schedule a more formal review of your calculations. And once we get everything verified, we can start thinking about the next steps."

Mark shook hands with the other professors, feeling a sense of relief but also an enormous weight of responsibility beginning to settle on his shoulders. This was real now. His theory, which had been just a collection of scribbles in a notebook, was about to become something much bigger. The work had only just begun.

As he left the university, the crisp autumn air hit his face, cooling the flush of excitement on his cheeks. Mark took a moment to breathe in deeply, feeling the reality of the situation start to sink in. The world he had always felt distant from—the world of science and discovery—was now opening up to him. He had no idea what would come next, but for the first time, he believed that his ideas might actually change the way humanity understood the universe.

But even with that thrill coursing through him, something nagged at the back of his mind. His family. Sarah, Penny, the kids. He had spent the past few weeks consumed by his work, distracted, distant. They needed him too. It wasn't just the professors and the equations pulling at him now; it was his life at home, the people he loved most. How was he going to balance it all?

As he drove home, the excitement of the day began to give way to a creeping sense of doubt.

He had just taken the first step toward something huge, but the cost—if he wasn't careful—could be more than he realized.

Chapter 4: Seeking Recognition

By the time Mark pulled into the driveway that evening, the sky had darkened, and the glow from the house's windows felt warm and inviting. He stepped inside to the familiar chaos of home: the kids were running around, Sarah was cooking dinner, and Penny was drawing at the kitchen table.

"Daddy!" Penny called, jumping up to greet him. "I drew a picture of a black hole! Just like the ones you talk about!"

Mark smiled as Penny held up her drawing—an imaginative swirl of dark crayon with stars scattered around it. He knelt down to her level, marveling at how her mind worked, even at such a young age.

"That's amazing, Penny," he said, pulling her into a hug. "You're going to be a scientist one day, I just know it."

Penny beamed, her bright eyes lighting up as she held her picture proudly. It was moments like this, simple and joyful, that grounded Mark.

Despite the weight of everything that was happening, this was his real life—his children, his wife, his family. They were his universe.

Sarah appeared from the kitchen, wiping her hands on a dish towel. "You're home late," she said, giving him a curious look.

"Yeah, sorry about that," Mark replied, standing up. "I… I had a meeting. With some professors at Ohio University."

Sarah raised an eyebrow. "Professors? About what?"

Mark hesitated. How could he explain what had just happened without it sounding insane? He took a deep breath and decided to be direct.

"About my theory," he said. "The one I've been working on. They're interested in it. They want to collaborate with me."

Sarah stared at him, her expression unreadable. For a moment, Mark feared she might not believe him, that she'd laugh it off or think he was exaggerating.

But instead, she blinked in surprise. "Wait… seriously?"

"Yeah," Mark said, nodding. "They think I'm onto something. They're going to review my calculations, and if everything checks out, they want to work with me."

Sarah was quiet for a moment, processing the news. Finally, she smiled—a slow, warm smile that filled Mark with relief. "That's incredible, Mark. I mean, I knew you were working on something, but I didn't realize…this is huge." Mark grinned, feeling the tension in his chest loosen. "It is. I'm still trying to wrap my head around it."

She stepped closer, putting a hand on his arm. "I'm proud of you. Really. I know how much this means to you."

Mark felt a surge of gratitude. For all his late nights, his absences, Sarah had been patient. She had supported him even when she didn't fully understand what he was doing. Now, for the first time, it felt like she could see just how important this was.

"Thank you," he said softly. "I couldn't have done it without you."

Sarah smiled again, but this time there was a hint of weariness in her eyes. "Just…don't forget about us, okay? I know this is a big deal, but the kids still need their dad. I still need you."

Mark's heart sank a little. He hadn't meant to neglect them, but he knew she was right. In his excitement, he had let himself become consumed by the work, by the allure of solving the universe's mysteries. But in doing so, he had started to drift away from the very people who gave his life meaning.

"I won't," Mark promised. "I'm going to find a way to make this work, without losing sight of what's important."

Sarah nodded, her expression softening. "I know you will. I believe in you."

They shared a quiet moment, the weight of the day hanging between them. But there was hope there too, a sense that they could navigate this new chapter together, even if the road ahead was uncertain.

Over the next few weeks, Mark's life became a balancing act. The professors at Ohio University had sent him a steady stream of feedback and questions about his theory, asking him to refine certain points and clarify others. Mark spent his evenings working on the revisions, poring over the math, while trying to stay present for his family during the day.

It wasn't easy. Some nights, after the kids were asleep, he would sit at his desk for hours, the numbers swimming in front of his eyes as fatigue pulled at him. Other nights, when

Sarah asked him to watch a movie with her or help the kids with homework, he would catch himself thinking about the equations, his mind drifting even as he tried to focus on family life.

But he kept his promise to Sarah, doing his best to maintain the balance. He was still present for school runs, for family dinners, for bedtime stories. And yet, there was always a part of him that couldn't fully detach from the work. The theory had taken root in his mind, and it demanded attention, pulling at him like gravity.

One evening, just as he was wrapping up a revision of one of his equations, his phone buzzed with a new email. It was from Dr. Jameson.

Mark opened it quickly, his pulse quickening. The subject line read: Initial Review Results.

He scanned the email, his heart pounding in his chest. The professors had completed the initial review of his theory, running the equations through various tests and models. And the results… the results were promising.

Mark's hands shook as he read the final paragraph:

"Your theory continues to hold under scrutiny. We believe it has the potential to revolutionize our understanding of black holes and the nature of spacetime. We would like to move forward with a formal presentation to the wider academic community. Please let us know your availability for further discussions."

Mark sat back in his chair, staring at the screen. It was happening. His theory was gaining real traction, and now the next step was within reach—a formal presentation, recognition from the academic community. This was everything he had worked for, everything he had dreamed of.

But as the excitement surged through him, so did the familiar tug of doubt. The deeper he went into this world, the more it pulled him away from the life he had built with Sarah and the kids. Could he really balance both worlds? Could he chase this dream without losing everything else?

For now, there were no answers. Only the pull of the work, and the gravity of the choices he had yet to make.

<u>Chapter 5: Academic Validation</u>

Mark sat in his office, staring at the blinking cursor on his screen. The email from Dr. Jameson had arrived two days ago, confirming that his theory had passed the initial review. Since then, he hadn't been able to think about much else. He had tried to go about his regular routine—helping the kids with homework, fixing a few cars in the garage—but his mind was elsewhere. He kept replaying the words in the email: Your theory continues to hold under scrutiny… revolutionize our understanding of black holes and the nature of spacetime.

He had spent the last few weeks sending back revisions, clarifying parts of the theory that the professors had questioned. Every time they responded, the feedback was positive, their curiosity deepening. It was like a slow avalanche gaining momentum. They were preparing him for something big—a formal presentation to the academic community. It wasn't just his idea anymore; it was becoming real, validated by people who had devoted their lives to physics.

The house was quiet now. Sarah had taken the kids out for the afternoon, giving him time to work. But despite the stillness, Mark couldn't focus. His thoughts were racing. He knew that soon, maybe in a matter of weeks, he would stand in front of some of the brightest minds in the world and present his work. A work that had been born in the solitude of his basement late at night, scrawled across the pages of an old notebook.

And they would be there, all of them— peers, professors, physicists, experts. People who had spent decades studying the very topics Mark had stumbled upon. What if they asked him questions he couldn't answer? What if they exposed flaws in his calculations that he hadn't seen?

The fear was gnawing at him now. What if all of this attention—the collaboration, the reviews, the meetings—was leading up to a moment where he would fail?

He sighed, leaning back in his chair. As much as he tried to suppress it, the feeling of inadequacy lingered. He was just a mechanic. He hadn't even finished his degree. He hadn't studied at the great universities, hadn't spent years doing research. How could he stand in front of these people and claim to have discovered something that could change their understanding of the universe?

Mark stood and began pacing the small office. The afternoon sunlight filtered through the basement window, casting long shadows on the floor. His notebook lay open on the desk, the pages filled with equations, diagrams, and half-formed thoughts. He glanced at it, wondering if he had made a mistake in sending it to Dr. Jameson in the first place. Maybe it had been a fluke, and he had just gotten lucky with a few pieces of math that happened to fit together.

He had been so focused on the math, so consumed by the theory, that he hadn't stopped to think about what it would mean if this became his life. What would happen to his family? To his relationship with Sarah and the kids? He had promised Sarah that he wouldn't let the work take over, but that promise felt harder to keep with every passing day.

The familiar sound of the front door creaking open snapped him out of his thoughts. Sarah's voice floated down from upstairs. "Mark? We're back!"

Mark made his way up the stairs to find the kids bustling through the living room, carrying grocery bags and chattering about their day. Penny, as usual, was the first to run over to him, her face beaming.

"Daddy! Guess what? I found a book about stars! It's got pictures of black holes and everything!" Penny thrust the book toward him, her excitement palpable.

Mark smiled, ruffling her hair. "That's awesome, Penny. We'll have to read it together later."

She skipped off happily, and Mark turned to see Sarah in the kitchen, unpacking groceries. She glanced at him with a knowing smile, wiping her hands on a towel. "How's the work going?" she asked.

Mark hesitated for a moment, then shrugged. "It's… going. They want me to give a formal presentation soon. To the academic community."

Sarah raised an eyebrow, pausing in her work. "That's amazing, Mark. But you don't seem as excited as I thought you'd be."

Mark let out a long breath, leaning against the counter. "I don't know. I guess I'm just…nervous. What if I get up there and they tear the whole thing apart? What if it's all just…wrong?"

Sarah stepped closer, placing a hand on his arm. "Mark, you've been working on this for months. You've put everything you have into it. And from what you've told me, the professors think you're onto something real. You have to trust yourself."

"I know," Mark muttered, though he wasn't sure he believed it.

Sarah looked at him for a moment, her eyes soft with understanding. "I know this is a big deal, but just remember—whatever happens, you have us. This theory is important, but it's not the only thing that matters."

Mark nodded, feeling a rush of gratitude for her support. Sarah had been the one to ground him through all of this, to remind him that his family was the anchor that kept him from floating off into the abyss of equations and theoretical physics. He knew she was right, but it didn't make the upcoming presentation any less daunting.

The weeks that followed were a whirlwind of preparation. The professors at Ohio University helped him refine his presentation, guiding him on how to explain the complexities of his theory in a way that would resonate with the academic audience. They arranged for him to present at a regional physics conference, a gathering of respected scientists and researchers who were eager to hear about his work.

As the day of the presentation approached, Mark found himself torn between excitement and terror. The theory was sound, the math checked out, and the feedback from the professors had been overwhelmingly positive. But still, the fear lingered. What if he wasn't good enough? What if the audience saw him for what he truly was—a mechanic with no formal education, trying to claim a seat at a table he didn't belong to?

On the morning of the presentation, Mark woke up early, unable to sleep. He went through his routine in a daze, showering, getting dressed, and grabbing a quick breakfast before heading to the conference. Sarah had kissed him on the cheek before he left, whispering, "You've got this," in his ear.

But even as he drove to the venue, his hands gripped the steering wheel tightly, his mind buzzing with anxiety.

The conference center was large and imposing, filled with scientists and researchers from all over the region. As Mark entered the lobby, he was struck by the sheer scale of it all— booths filled with research papers, presentations being set up in various rooms, groups of people deep in discussion. He felt like an outsider, a visitor in a world that wasn't his.

Dr. Jameson met him in the lobby, his face calm and reassuring. "Are you ready, Mark?" he asked, clapping him on the shoulder.

"As ready as I'll ever be," Mark replied, trying to keep the tremble out of his voice.

They made their way to the lecture hall where Mark would be giving his presentation. The room was large, with rows of seats that were quickly filling with attendees. Mark set up his materials at the front of the room, adjusting the projector and arranging his notes on the podium.

He glanced around the room, seeing the faces of the audience—professors, students, researchers. Some of them had probably been studying black holes and cosmology for decades. What would they think of him? Would they even listen?

As the last of the attendees settled into their seats, Dr. Jameson introduced him, giving a brief overview of Mark's background and his work. And then, before he knew it, Mark was standing at the podium, facing the crowd.

His heart pounded in his chest as he began speaking, his voice shaky at first. He outlined the basics of his theory—the idea that black holes were not isolated phenomena but the fundamental building blocks of the universe. He explained the concept of collapse expansion dynamics, how black holes might act as nodes in a web of dimensional interactions, influencing everything from quantum mechanics to the structure of spacetime itself.

At first, he was afraid to look up, afraid of seeing skeptical faces or disinterested expressions. But as he went on, something remarkable happened. The crowd was listening. Really listening. He could see it in their eyes—their attention focused on him, their curiosity piqued. Some were even nodding along, scribbling notes, leaning forward in their seats.

As he moved into the more technical aspects of the theory, his confidence grew. The equations, the patterns—they all made sense. And the audience seemed to understand that, too. There were no signs of dismissal, no skeptical smirks or condescending glances. Just a room full of people who were genuinely interested in what he had to say.

When he finished, the room was silent for a moment, as if the audience was processing everything he had just shared. And then, to Mark's astonishment, the room erupted into applause.

Mark stood there, stunned, as the applause echoed in the hall. Dr. Jameson beamed at him from the side of the stage, and the other professors who had worked with him nodded in approval. The feeling of validation washed over Mark like a wave.

For the first time in months, he felt a profound sense of accomplishment. His work was real. It mattered. And for a moment, he allowed himself to believe that he truly belonged in this world.

Excerpts From
Forthcoming Prose

Josh Greenbaum

excerpt from
Crow and Coyote
Save the World

"Where the hell did he come from?" Crow was almost hysterical. "What if he'd had a gun? What was he doing there?"

"I don't know, I only saw him when he popped out of the tent. I guess he had been in there all the time." Melody was jogging easily alongside Coyote, the two canids following Crow as they headed downriver towards the washed-out dam.

"If he was there the whole time, why the hell didn't you smell him out? Isn't that what you nose jobs are supposed to be good at?" Crow was flitting around nervously, looking more like a swallow on the wing than a crow.

"We did smell him – there was this strong stench of cow shit and human shit the moment we arrived. I just assumed the cow shit smell was from the cattle grazing nearby and the human shit was from the toilet. No one expected the two scents to be coming from some guy sleeping in his tent." Coyote was trying to keep an eye on Crow as he spoke. She was still bobbing around too much to make it easy.

"Classic diversionary tactic," Melody said sarcastically. "Roll around in your prey's shit and then if they catch wind of you, you smell like them instead like an alpha predator. But by then you're right on top of them and have already launched your attack. Must have been here for the annual cow hunt."

"Cow hunt?" Coyote said, tilting his head towards Melody, looking perplexed. "They hunt cows?" Crow was having none of it. "Humans don't roll in cow shit so they can hunt cows, and they definitely don't perfume it with some of their own. They just walk up to them and shoot; the cows are way too stupid to know they're supposed to run away. Whatever he was doing smelling like that, this guy got way too close, and he definitely got a good look at us. You know that beaver told us to stay away from humans, as if getting shot at a couple of weeks ago wasn't a good enough reason to avoid them."

The three companions stopped suddenly; all heads turned back towards the campsite. Even though they were a ways down the hill, heading towards the sloping mudflats that defined the edges of the former lake bed, they could hear the crunching of truck tires on the road behind them. They waited, still enough to hear the light breeze rustling up from the water below. The skidding sound of the truck tires as the driver hit the brakes was reassuring – the truck had definitely stopped – and so they continued in silence down the hill and then skirted along the lake's former shoreline, now the outer perimeter of a sloping muddy mess leading to a gentle, newly free-flowing Bear River. Crow relaxed a bit as they put some distance between them and the parking lot, taking comfort in the fact that both her companions were relatively well-camouflaged in this scrub brush and sage terrain. She led them to the western side of what used to be the dam and its access road - the dam failure had carved it into a sharp cliffside overlooking the ravaged canyon. Melody and Coyote just stared down at the mess below, wordless. Crow finally broke the silence.

"It's not all devastation and destruction, wait till you see what's happening around that bend in the river ahead." From that angle they could see the edge of the new beaver pond peaking around the corner, though only Crow knew what that flat water meant. She took flight and led them over the hillside to where they could safely drop down into the new riverbed below.

Beckett and Ari pulled into the Golden Spike Visitor Center when the message popped up, dusk looming in the sky behind them. The run from the Visitor Center to the Spiral Jetty, or more accurately, to where the Spiral Jetty used to be, had crossed a barren land devoid of pretty much everything, including cellphone coverage. The national park system had wifi coverage as part of its services, apparently. "Can you meet me at Woodruff Reservoir tomorrow?" It was from Booch.

"How far is Woodruff Reservoir from here," Beckett asked as Ari jammed the Scout into park and then grabbed their Utah road atlas and started thumbing through the index. "I've got a Woodruff Cooperative Wildlife-Livestock Management Area, page 16, H1." He started flipping the pages. "I'm guessing that's it, right near a town called Woodruff in southeast Wyoming and there's what looks like a lake or reservoir on the Bear River right there."

Beckett was already trying to get her map app up. The wifi, such as it was, wasn't the swiftest, and it took a few seconds to find Woodruff and calculate the distance. Just outside of Woodruff, due east and a tad south, was the Woodruff Reservoir. "Just under two hours," Beckett announced, and looked over at Ari. "Shall we head over?"

"Do you want to maybe call him and ask him why? And why don't we first head into Salt Lake and grab some dinner and sleep in our completely over-furnished and underused apartment. We can go over in the morning if it makes sense." He looked over, glanced at his wife, and realized going anywhere but straight to Woodruff was a lost cause. Ari smiled at the blank face and bright, almost fiery eyes staring back at him and tried again. "How about I'll head us over to Woodruff, you call Booch and find out what's up, and then figure out a hotel and dinner somewhere nearby?"

Beckett smiled and nodded, then squeezed his hand and looked back at her phone. "Get us back to I-84, and then head south to the I-80 interchange and then head north."

"Don't you want to at least take a look at the Visitor Center? Maybe they have a nice hat I can add to my collection?"

He stared down at the blank face and fiery eyes again, which then softened into a broad smile. "Sure, you only have like 30 national and state park hats, let's get you number 31. Anyway, I gotta pee."

Despite the relatively fine day, the windows were up and the AC was on as they headed back down highway 83 towards Brigham City and the freeway. It was the only way the aftermarket sound system Ari had installed in the Scout would be clear enough to hear a phone call, and Booch had just picked up the phone.

"There's a few things I think you should see over at Woodruff," Booch was explaining. "It's kind of exciting."

"Where are you now?" Ari shouted into the microphone hidden somewhere on the dash.

"I'm camped in the little Wyoming Game and Fish campground near what used to be Woodruff Reservoir, now basically a rewilded leg of Bear River since the dam went out. I decided I should poke around and see what I could see for myself. Turns out there's lots to see. And smell."

"Care to give us some clues?" It was Beckett's turn to shout.

"I'd rather just show you, when do you think you'll be here?"

"We're grabbing a hotel and something eat in Evanston, we'll leave at first light and head over to you." Beckett glanced over at Ari and saw his eyebrows raise up at the words "first light." "Or maybe even earlier," she said for effect, and got a swat on the shoulder from Ari. "Seriously – the hotel has a free breakfast and I'm counting on some make-your-own waffles and bacon to power me through the day. It's only thirty minutes away. I figure we'll be there by 8:30 or so." Ari smiled and blew her a kiss.

"I should tell you about Spiral Jetty," Beckett continued. "It's underwater again."

"Wow, that's kind of cool. Do you know long has it been since the lake was that high?"

"Twelve years, we just looked it up on the Dia Foundation website. There was water almost up to the access road. We climbed up the hill to the little marker and took some pictures. The Jetty was sort of ghost-like under the water. I forgot how beautiful it could be with all that red water and foam around it. We had just gotten back to Golden Spike when we got your text."

"Did you go inside? Tell me they finally figured out a way to have a concession there that sells coffee, they could make a goddamn mint – it wouldn't have to be any good and it would still be the only coffee west of Corinne."

"Not a chance. We just crossed the Bear River at Corinne, by the way, lots of flooded fields and mud. Doesn't look like any real property damage, at least anything visible from the road."

"No property damage unless it's your ranch under all that mud. They're still cleaning out the mess at the Bird Refuge visitor center I hear. A few tons of standing muck and debris for a good couple of days makes a helluva cleanup problem."

The next morning, hyped up on carbs, bacon, and two cups of pretty decent coffee, Beckett steered the Scout off the main road out of Evanston and on to the dirt track that led up to Bear River Access area. Booch had told them to drive until they saw the small outhouse halfway down to the water. About a mile in, Beckett stopped on a rise looking over the mudflats and newly freed river to get her bearings, and she and Ari stepped out to take a look. To their right, looming in the mist in the distance, was the escarpment that announced the beginning of the Uinta Mountains: Somewhere up there a little lake, fed by rivulets of snowmelt in the spring and trickles of burbling ground water the rest of the year, was the source of the Bear River that now flowed freely in the valley below. Closer at hand was a marshy wetland at the south end of the washed-out lake. Clumps of what had been partially submerged bushes now loomed atop islands of muck and roots sticking out of the former lakebed, and small fingers of water meandered through newly-carved mud gullies, trying to find a way to navigate the chaos of the drained lake and reform as part of the river. A glance through the binoculars showed a variety of birds flitting through the greenery or padding around in the mud – redwing blackbirds, ducks, mergansers, and a few she didn't recognize. A phalanx of white pelicans, their black-tipped underwings highlighting bright white wings against a cerulean sky, wheeled in the distance. A dam may have been destroyed – but to Beckett and Ari, nature seemed not just unscathed, but gloriously triumphant.

They pulled into the parking lot near the toilets, and saw two tents set up on the perimeter. One, a neat orange tent with a camping kitchen and table, and camp chair set up at its side, was the home of Booch, who looked up from a book as they pulled in and got to his feet. His forest green 4x4 truck, white plastic water tanks screwed to the side of its camper top, a kayak and a mountain bike on the roof rack, was parked nearby. The other was a motley lime-green tent, somewhat disheveled, with a red non-descript SUV at its side. A man sitting in a camp chair watched as they pulled in, and then got up to busy himself with something on the other side of the tent.

"Welcome to the former Woodruff Narrows Reservoir. Maybe it's now more appropriate to just call it Woodruff Narrows. Or, to be even more succinct: the newly rewilded Bear River. Ain't she a beaut?" Booch opened his arms grandiosely, and embraced his two friends. "Sorry about the smell, though. There were a lot of dead fish in the reservoir after the dam blew – species that can only live in reservoir-like conditions, individuals stranded on the newly former shore. There's been a bit of a feeding frenzy, so most of the dead fish and the smell are gone, relatively speaking." He smiled again and wrinkled his nose.

The man near the green tent started ambling over - it was clear he wanted something from them, and when he got about ten feet away the three friends stopped their greetings and turned to face their visitor. He was wearing a light blue shirt that was stained on the front and barely tucked into a pair of dusty jeans, his hair longish and matted, his boots more dusty than his jeans and cracked across the top of the toe box. He smiled sheepishly – it was a kind, beery smile, it was clear he meant no harm, and could hardly cause any if he tried.

Booch smiled and spoke first. "How you doing? Everything ok?"

The man smiled again. "Been a while since everything was ok, to be honest. Anyone got a smoke?"

"No smokers here," Booch answered, "sorry."

"How long you've been camping here," Ari thought he was being conversational, but the man's response surprised him.

"Depends on who's asking," was the reply. "You're not with Game and Fish, are you?"

"Oh no," Ari replied gently. "Why?"

"You see, you're only allowed to be here for two weeks," the man gestured to the sign near the outhouse. "So I had to leave two days ago, just came back yesterday. Not sure if you could come back in just a day and have a whole 'nother two weeks."

Booch's demeanor shifted instantly. "Two weeks? Were you here two weeks ago? When the dam went out?"

"Oh shit yeah," the man replied. "That was a crazy night. Real crazy."

The three friends all looked at each other and then at the man. "What's your name?" Beckett said softly.

"Joe."

"Hi Joe, I'm Beckett, this is my husband Ari, and that's our friend, Booch. Booch, you think you could make some coffee for Joe and the rest of us?" She turned and looked at Joe, smiling warmly. "Booch makes great coffee."

"Ma'am, I would drink coffee made from shoe leather right now if you gave it to me."

...

"So there was no explosion of any kind?" Beckett was trying her best to make this a gentle interrogation, but it was hard keeping Joe's rambling storyline in check.

"Nope, but when that big wad of trees and junk hit the top of the dam, it made a pretty loud crunching sound."

"What wad of trees?"

"Right before the dam broke, this huge bunch of trees – it looked as big as an island and all tangled and twisted – came floating down the reservoir and bounced right square into the center of the dam. Made a weird crunching sound. The rain had stopped by then, but the water just kept rising. Then that mess of trees and stuff got caught in an eddy and started spinning, but it was too big, and it floated over to the top of the spillway and stuck there like a big old cork."

"How tall was this mess of trees?" Booch had his brow furrowed and was obviously thinking hard about something.

"I dunno, it was tall as…" Joe stopped and sucked his coffee, smiling. He took another sip, smiled again, and sighed. Booch's gourmet cowboy coffee was doing the trick. "Must've been eight, ten feet tall. More. It jammed up the spillway completely, and was still way above the level of the dam."

"Any big trees? Or just brush and stuff?" Booch was on to something.

"Big trees, little trees, brush – just looked like a big-ass tangle to me."

"And the water level in the dam started rising, right, because it couldn't go down the spillway anymore? And then it began overtopping the dam itself?" Booch was having trouble containing his excitement.

"If by overtopping you mean water that couldn't go down the spillway started just going over the dam, yep. But you know what was weird? It didn't do that for too long and then all of a sudden it looked like someone had punched the dam in the gut, and it collapsed in from the center.

One second there was water going over the top, and the next second the center of the dam sort of imploded from under the lake, and the sides folded up and followed the rest of the dam into the canyon. That big plug of trees got caught in the current and was sucked out of the spillway and went down into the canyon with the rest of the dam. It was scary as hell, I wasn't sure I was safe sitting up way on a bluff an easy 150 feet away.

"I've been here ever since, and then the two weeks were up and the ranger kicked me out. That was the day I saw a coyote and some big dog here, right under the sign over there."

"A coyote and a dog?" Beckett looked over, trying to hide her surprise. "Together? What did the dog look like?"

"Big and bushy, kind of like a small bear. I would've gotten a better look but this stupid crow dive-bombed me and I fell over into my tent." Joe had that sheepish, beery grin again.

Beckett and Ari looked at each other, and then at Booch. "A crow?"

"A goddamn crow near hit me on the head. Lucky I dodged it. When I got back up the three of them were gone."